DISASTER DIARIES

THE WORST BIRTHDAY EVER

Daffodil
Madrigal
Mum
Lupin
Grandma
Dad
Colin

Aunt Rex
Uncle Malcolm
Muriel
Hugo
Nirmal
Tonks
Ariel

Books by Joanna Nadin

The Worst Class in the World series

The Worst Class in the World

The Worst Class in the World
Gets Worse

The Worst Class in the World
Dares You!

The Worst Class in the World
Goes Wild!

The Worst Class in the World:
Total Mayhem!

The Worst Class in the World:
Animal Uproar

Disaster Diaries:
The Worst Birthday Ever

DISASTER DIARIES

JOANNA NADIN

ILLUSTRATED BY
RIKIN PAREKH

THE WORST BIRTHDAY EVER

BLOOMSBURY
CHILDREN'S BOOKS
LONDON OXFORD NEW YORK NEW DELHI SYDNEY

BLOOMSBURY CHILDREN'S BOOKS
Bloomsbury Publishing Plc
50 Bedford Square, London WC1B 3DP, UK
29 Earlsfort Terrace, Dublin 2, Ireland

BLOOMSBURY, BLOOMSBURY CHILDREN'S BOOKS and the Diana logo
are trademarks of Bloomsbury Publishing Plc

First published in Great Britain in 2025 by Bloomsbury Publishing Plc

A catalogue record for this book is available from the British Library

ISBN: PB: 978-1-5266-7558-3; eBook: 978-1-5266-7557-6;
ePDF: 978-1-5266-7555-2

2 4 6 8 10 9 7 5 3 1

Printed and bound in Great Britain by CPI Group (UK) Ltd, Croydon CR0 4YY

FSC www.fsc.org
MIX
Paper | Supporting responsible forestry
FSC® C171272

To find out more about our authors and books visit www.bloomsbury.com
and sign up for our newsletters

For Paul, my best BOBBY DAZZLER

– J.N.

For Olive, Tom and Todd, Adani's WONDERFUL godparents

– R.P.

This diary belongs to:

Daffodil Patterson

Age: 8 (nearly)

Height: 107cm (which Madrigal, i.e. my big sister, who is thirteen and who is mostly protesting about things, says is **UNUSUALLY** short and so I am **SMALL FRY**. But I say she is **UNUSUALLY** annoying)

Hair colour: Brownish

Eye colour: Brownish

Likes:

a) Pangolins (which are STRANGE and ENDANGERED, and look a bit like this):

b) Nirmal-Next-Door (who is my best friend, because we agree about everything except the best flavour of crisp, which he says is Beefy Hoops and I say is Cheesy Frizzles and I am right).

3. The biscuit bit of a custard cream

(but not the middle,
but that is OK
because Nirmal
eats that).

4. BOBBY DAZZLERS, which means brilliant ideas (because Dad says ANYONE can have a BOBBY DAZZLER, i.e. look at Aunt Rex, who once had a BOBBY DAZZLER about photocopiers and now her house is massive and has a fridge with a drinks dispenser and a pedigree cat called Juniper who only eats minced fish. Our house, i.e. 43 Bean Street is SQUISHED and we

do not have ONE pet, although Lupin, who is my big brother, is quite hairy and smells of STALE).

e) Lists.

Dislikes:

a) Wasps (because they look like bees but aren't and Nirmal says they are always UP TO SOMETHING and I agree).

2. Slow worms (because they look like snakes but aren't and Nirmal says they are probably UP TO SOMETHING and I agree).

3. Being the smallest in our house because hardly anyone listens to me and sometimes I am UTTERLY forgotten.

4. Hugo Patterson-Dent (i.e. my cousin, because he is mostly saying things like 'I would not do THAT if I were you, Daffodil Patterson'. And I do THAT and he is right).

e) When BOBBY DAZZLERS go wrong (see 4) and Grandma calls us CATASTROPHE PATTERSONS and does a snort like a broken vacuum cleaner.

Aunt Rex says the going wrong is because of **ALL THE MAYHEM** at 43 Bean Street, and Mum says it is because me and Dad **DO NOT KNOW OUR LIMITS**, but I say I just need a better **BOBBY DAZZLER** and I will probably have one tomorrow.

Saturday

3ish

It is the **FIRST** day of the school holidays, which is normally **AMAZING** because me and Nirmal can **FOOTLE** all we like, which means **BIMBLE**, which means **HAVE FUN** by not doing anything very much. But it is also **FOUR** days until my birthday and not **ONE** person has even **MENTIONED** it yet. This is because it is **NORMAL SERVICE** at 43 Bean Street, i.e. everyone is ignoring me. Dad is busy being a postman, Mum is busy at Glory Days Care Home with all the old people, Lupin is busy with his band in the **LAIR**, i.e. the shed, Madrigal is busy being **ANNOYING**, and Grandma is busy **MINDING HER OWN BUSINESS**, i.e. reading the newspapers and saying things like 'the world is a terrible place'.

But if we say she is wrong and the world is quite nice (e.g. what about chocolate cake and pangolins?) she says, 'You should be kinder to me, I could be **GONE** tomorrow.' And I do not know where, but she never is.

Nirmal says I should just **ASK** about my birthday, because one of

his mums, i.e. Call-Me-Ariel, says it is important to be **CLEAR ABOUT YOUR NEEDS**. This is because she is a **THERAPIST**, i.e. she mainly has long talks in her office with gloomy-looking people and then they go away looking less gloomy and smelling of candle. I am going to be clear about my needs in the kitchen right now.

4ish

Being clear did not go exactly to plan. When I got into the kitchen Mum was arguing with Dad about when he was going to fix the **LAIR** (which she says is about to collapse and which he says has a 'good life ahead of it yet') and Lupin was staring into the fridge because he is always hungry, and Madrigal was yelling at Lupin for wasting electricity because he is **LITERALLY** killing polar bears every time he can't decide whether he wants cheese or hummus.

I did a cough and said, 'For

my birthday on Wednesday …'

But not **ONE** person even noticed me. So I said it louder and **STILL** not **ONE** person even noticed me. So I stood on a chair and said it **REALLY LOUD** and that is when it went wrong, i.e. Mum said, 'What birthday?' and Dad said, 'Ooops!' and Madrigal said, '**LITERALLY** dying!' but that was to Lupin again.

I said, '**I CANNOT** believe not **ONE** of you has remembered it is my birthday,' because that was being very **CLEAR**. And also, 'I bet

Aunt Rex has not forgotten it is Hugo's birthday tomorrow.'

And then it became **CLEAR** that they had all forgotten it was Hugo's (i.e. my cousin's) birthday too and Mum said she did not have time to get a present because of a crisis at Glory Days with Mavis Battenburg, so Dad said **HE** would get something.

Mum said, 'Do not spend a packet, Marv.'

So Grandma did one of her faces and said, 'You should have been

more like

your brother.'

Because

Dad's brother

is Uncle

Malcolm,

who is married to Aunt Rex, who is a **PHOTOCOPIER MAGNATE** (which is like a king only better) and has vans with her name on and also the fridge with the drinks dispenser.

Only Dad said, 'Quite happy being me, Ma, and **WHO IS TO SAY**

I won't make my fortune next week?'

Grandma looked like she was about to say it, only Dad said he was going to see Disco Dave, who is another postman (and also Chipping Grimley Ultimate Frisbee Champion), and who has a garage full of **BARGAINS** and he is often selling them to Dad, e.g.

1. Four dozen tins of baked beans.
2. A Cats of the World calendar with only November missing.

c) A soup machine.

I asked if I could come, because I quite like it at Disco Dave's house because of all the **BARGAINS** and also because he teaches me Frisbee tricks and no one tells me off if I, e.g. knock over a vase or get the Frisbee caught on top of a wardrobe, but Mum said no I could not, it was bad enough that Dad was going. And then Lupin moaned that he was only staring into the fridge because Madrigal and Luna (i.e. her best friend, who only wears black and looks a bit like a bat) have eaten all the custard creams, so I have decided to go to Nirmal's, because he is an **ONLY** child and so his house is full of **PEACE**, and also biscuits.

6ish

Dad is always telling me to look on the **BRIGHT** side of things because there is always something to be happy about. So, on the **BRIGHT** side, Me and Nirmal have written a birthday present list and it is a **BOBBY DAZZLER**:

a) A pet (any kind, but preferably a pangolin, a pigeon or a raven who can talk).

2. Rocket boots.

c) A World of Wizard helmet of invisibility.

On the **GLOOM** side, Mum says I cannot have a pangolin because they are **STRANGE** and also **ENDANGERED**, or a pigeon because they do not know what is a toilet and what isn't, or a raven who can talk because it is too noisy round here already. Also I cannot have rocket boots because they are not real, but I can have some new flip-flops as long as I do not do what I did last time and flip-flop them up and down the kitchen for five hours because I like the sound. I said I would try.

Then Nirmal said, 'What about the **PET SITUATION**, Mrs Patterson?'

And Mum did a sigh and said, 'I will **THINK** about it.'

Nirmal said this is a **GOOD SIGN** and probably I will get a hamster or a chinchilla or some sea monkeys, because he is **VERY KEEN** on sea monkeys.

I do not know where I would keep a sea monkey because the bath is **OUT OF ACTION** until Dad fixes the plug (which he says will be 'very shortly' and Mum says it had better be) so it is **SHOWERS ONLY**, but I wouldn't mind a hamster.

Sunday

10ish

Today is Hugo Patterson-Dent's birthday party and so I am **FULL OF GLOOM** because:

1. Nirmal is not invited because it is FAMILY and MATRAVERS SCHOOL only, and Nirmal goes to my school,

i.e. King Arthur Primary.

2. Hugo is bound to get ELEVENTY BILLION presents and say, 'Look at what I have got, Daffodil Patterson. I bet you do not get one of these.'

c) I have to wear clothes that are SENSIBLE and SMART, and not a hat shaped like a unicorn or wellies made of sparkle or my jeans that Dad says are more hole than trouser and we have a bet on how long before one leg falls off.

Only I do not have anything **SENSIBLE** and **SMART** except for my school uniform (which still has bean juice on it from the time me and Nirmal tried to see how many baked beans you can fit into your mouth at once, and it is not a hundred), so Mum has given me one of Madrigal's old dresses with a belt around it. Madrigal says I look **WEIRD** because I am **SMALL FRY** but Mum says I look like a Victorian Explorer who might be about to find ancient curses, and also it is that or my bean-juice uniform so I am wearing the dress.

Also Mum and Dad have already had a **TO-DO**, i.e. an argument. **AMAZINGLY** it was not about Hugo's present, which Dad **DID** get off Disco Dave, and is a Junior Chemistry Set with some labels missing (only Dad says labels **DO NOT MATTER**). It was about who has to take me to the party, i.e. Mum said she cannot go because she has to take Lupin to Beef McKenzie's house for an emergency band meeting and Dad said he cannot go because he has to take himself to Disco Dave's for an emergency **SOMETHING** meeting. Mum said unless he can name the **SOMETHING** then he loses and Dad said he cannot name the **SOMETHING** as it is a **SECRET**.

I said, 'Can I come to the **SECRET EMERGENCY SOMETHING** meeting instead of the party?'

And Mum and Dad suddenly agreed, i.e. they both yelled '**NO!**' and then Mum reminded Dad that Uncle Malcolm is **HIS** brother so

Hugo's party is **HIS** responsibility so he lost and has to take me.

Grandma said, 'When I was a girl, people were **PLEASED** to be invited to parties.'

Dad said, 'None of those parties involved Rex.'

But Grandma had gone back to the newspapers by then.

<u>5 p.m.</u>

Now I am even **FULLER OF GLOOM** and so is Dad.

It is because Hugo had:

a) a chocolate fountain with marshmallows and strawberries to dip in it.

b) a cake in the shape of a trumpet (because he is learning to play one and Aunt Rex says he is a PRODIGY and Madrigal says he is a threat to world peace).

3. Animal Stan, who is a man with a llama, and you get to pat it and feed it carrots.

And everyone went '**OOH**' and took a carrot from a bucket and queued up to give it to the llama, who was called Tessa. Only by the time it got to my turn Tessa had eaten seventeen carrots and she did not want even a **TINY BIT** of another one because she was too busy doing a poo on the lawn, which is when Aunt Rex decided it was time for Animal Stan to leave.

I said, 'But llama poos aren't even **BAD** poos, they are only number five in the poo ranks.' Because me and Nirmal have made a chart.

Carrots

And then Muriel Patterson-Dent, i.e. Hugo's little sister (who Grandma says is **GOOD AS GOLD** and then gives me a hard stare), said, 'What is the **WORST** poo, Daffodil?'

And I was about to say it was dog or fox or cow with a bad tummy when Hugo said, 'Why do you look like a **STRANGE LADY**, Daffodil Patterson?'

I said, 'I do not, I look like a Victorian Explorer who might be about to find ancient curses.'

Only he said, 'You actually do not.'

And I said, 'Do.'

And he said, 'Do not.'

And I said, 'Do and **NO RETURNS**.' Which means he cannot say anything back to me not even a **NOISE** and so I was

TRIUMPHANT. Only then Aunt Rex said perhaps it was **PRESENT TIME** and Hugo agreed and he **DID** get eleventy billion presents including:

1. A chess set and all the pieces are endangered animals.

b) A World of Wizard helmet of invisibility.

c) A book of Best Inventors Ever.

4. A waterproof watch that is accurate to a NANOSECOND.

5. The Junior Chemistry Set.

And Aunt Rex said, 'Where are the labels, Marvin?'

And Dad said, 'The labels **DO NOT MATTER**, Rex. Do not worry, I will do a demonstration.' And Uncle Malcolm said he would help.

Aunt Rex's lips went **VERY THIN** and her face went **VERY RED** and she said, 'For crying out loud, mind the rug, it's **IRREPLACEABLE**.'

But Dad said not to worry, because he and Uncle Malcolm were very good at chemistry when they were at school and in fact **WHO IS TO SAY** they aren't **SECRET SCIENTISTS** and will invent something **RIGHT NOW**?

And amazingly Aunt Rex did not say it, and so Dad and Uncle Malcolm got all the tubes of liquid and the packets of powder and the big beaker out and began to do **EXPERIMENTING**.

First of all they mixed some white powder with some blue liquid and it did some **FIZZING** and everyone went, '**OOH**!'

Next of all they mixed some red powder with some silver liquid and it did some **POPPING** and everyone went, '**AAH**!'

Then they mixed both of those together in the big beaker and it turns out labels **DO MATTER** because it went **BANG** and exploded purple foam all over Dad and Uncle Malcolm and the **IRREPLACEABLE** rug.

And that is when Aunt Rex decided it might be time for me and Dad to leave too, so I didn't

even get to try the white chocolate fountain or the cake in the shape of a trumpet. And when I got home I asked Mum if I could have a chocolate fountain and a llama at my party and she said, ‘What party?’ So it is clear I am

UTTERLY FORGOTTEN again.

Also, Lupin is in a mood and it is because of his band, which is him and Beef McKenzie and Oscar Boggins.

Madrigal said, 'Is it because no one will let you play a concert because you are **NOT GOOD**?'

Lupin said no, it is because they cannot agree on a name.

Mum said, 'Again?' Because so far this month they have been:

1. The Boggins Boys.

b) The Boggins Boyz.

3. Vigorous Pigeon.

Only now Beef wants to change their name to Hairy Wasp and Lupin wants to change their name to Meat Parlour. I do not know what a Meat Parlour is and said so, but Lupin said you do not need to know, the point is to **IMAGINE**, so I did and it was **NOT GOOD**. And now everyone is arguing over which band name is better and no one wants to talk about my party, so I will go to Nirmal's in the morning and make a plan and then I will be **CLEAR** about my **NEEDS** again.

Monday

__4ish__

Nirmal's house is **AMAZING**, because as well as **PEACE** and **BISCUITS** it is also full of **SPACE** (because it is only three people instead of six) and **ART** (because his other mum, Tonks, is famous for painting wonky kettles and once a dead heron). Plus he is allowed to do what he wants because Call-Me-Ariel says self-expression is very important for **DEVELOPMENT OF THE MIND**. So we developed our minds for a bit by:

1. Dangling upside down off the back of the sofa to see if we do not fall off and we do.

b) Eating toast with jam AND peanut butter AND cauliflower pickle to see if it tastes nice and it does not.

c) Making a tower out of a colander, ten tins of soup and a plastic spatula to see if it does not collapse and it does.

And then we did my party plan, i.e.

Daffodil Patterson's Party Plan

1. Roger the Wild Animal Man (who is like Stan only he has a tarantula and a gecko).

b) Call-Me-Ariel's friend Bogdan, who can juggle knives and EAT FIRE while playing the harmonica.

3. A pink chocolate fountain with marshmallows and strawberries to dip in it.

d) A birthday cake with ten layers and five kinds of icing and in the shape of a pangolin.

And we are going to invite the **WHOLE CLASS** (even Beavis Meek who we are not speaking to until he admits that green is the best Tooty Chew flavour) and most of our road. And it means my party will be **SUPREME** and **UNBEATABLE** and Hugo will be **WILD** with jealousy and Grandma will not make the snort noise. And I am going to tell Mum and Dad now while they are still in good moods, i.e. before Madrigal gets back from Luna's and starts arguing over why we are having chicken for dinner because of it having a face (because she went vegetarian this morning).

7ish

I have not told Mum and Dad about my party plan yet, only it is not because of the chicken. It is because Dad had one of his **BOBBY DAZZLER** ideas when he got home from work (which he says he is often having because he is a **GENIUS**, only Mum says he is **NOT**,

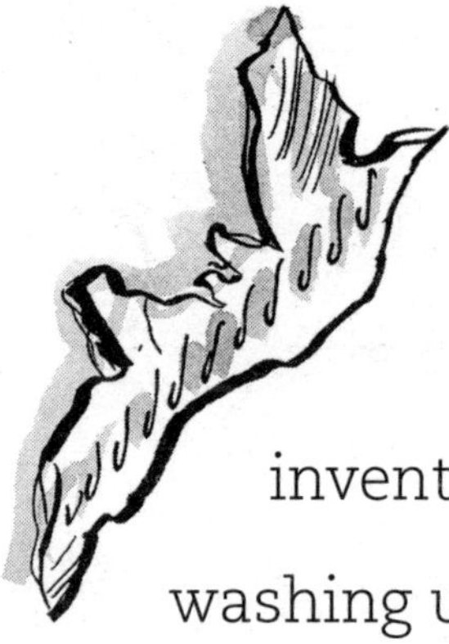

he is a **FOOLIGAN**) and this one was to invent a new way of washing up. Only he had broken all the plates and

a fancy glass and Mum's second-best mug, i.e. with the picture of a hippo on it, and so we had to eat our dinner out of four cereal bowls, a soup tureen and a saucepan. So now Dad has gone to Disco Dave's to see if

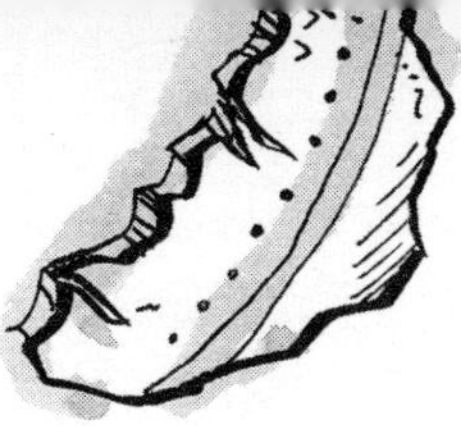

he has any plates in his

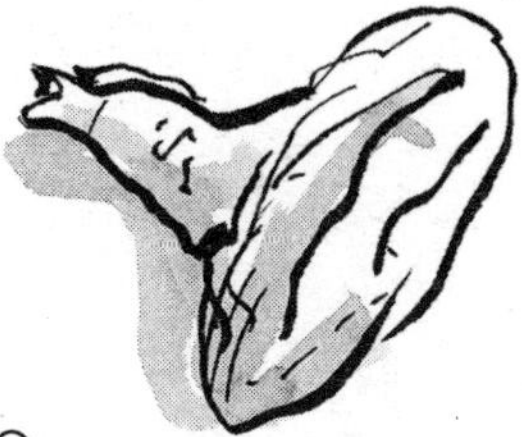

garage, Lupin has gone to Oscar Boggins's house to discuss the Meat Parlour crisis, and Mum and Madrigal are arguing over **UNSUITABLE SHOES** (because hers are made of **LEATHER**, which is not vegetarian, and she wants **ETHICAL** ones, but Mum says it is leather shoes or wellies or nothing).

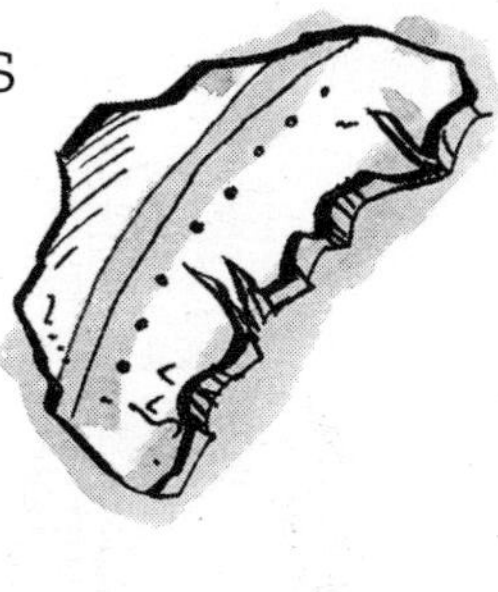

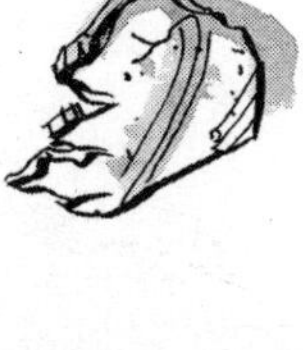

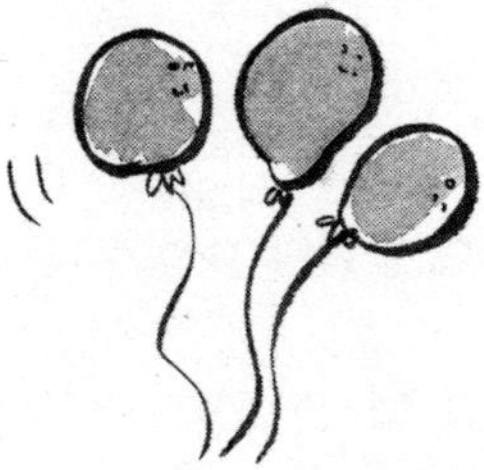

Tuesday

11 a.m.

I have still not told anyone about my party plan because I decided to go to Nirmal's super early and **DEVELOP MY MIND** by seeing what I look like with a felt-tip moustache (and also because he has Choco Pops cereal and we do not). By the time I got home there was **NO ONE** in except Grandma because Mum and Dad have gone to work, Lupin has gone to have it out with Beef McKenzie at Paradise City (which is the shop on the corner where Beef has a holiday job), and Madrigal and Luna have gone to **LURK** at Paradise City because they are both **OBSESSED** with Beef McKenzie. So now I will have to wait until teatime.

Also Grandma says the moustache reminds her of **HORACE MUNT** and I need to wash it off immediately. Only I cannot because Nirmal could not find his black felt-tip, he could only find a laundry pen, which is **INDELIBLE** and so it will not come off not even with **ALL THE SOAP**, so she says I am not allowed to look her in the eye for a while as it is **TOO UPSETTING**.

2ish

Me and Nirmal have added a beard but **NOW** Grandma says I look like **GIDEON FITZPATRICK**, which is **TEN TIMES WORSE**.

5ish

I have told Mum about my party plan. On the gloomy side, she said it cannot be on my actual birthday, i.e. Wednesday, because:

1. She will be at work and Dad is NOT TO BE TRUSTED to run a party on his own, not after last time.

b) Wednesday is tomorrow and that is not enough time to plan a THOUGHT let alone a party and perhaps I could have given her some more warning.

I said I had **TRIED** only everyone was too busy arguing about Meat Parlours and chickens and suitable shoes. And Mum said I should have **TRIED HARDER** because now it will be on Sunday, and no I cannot invite the **WHOLE CLASS** and most of the road, I can invite Nirmal, Call-Me-Ariel, Tonks, three friends from school, and Hugo and Muriel (or she will be in **BIG TROUBLE** with Aunt Rex). Plus I cannot have Roger, because Madrigal is scared of spiders, or Bogdan, because Grandma is allergic to the sound of harmonicas, or a chocolate fountain unless there is one in Dave's garage.

On the **BRIGHT** side, she says I **CAN** have a cake, only it will be in the shape of whatever she can get at short notice from Barry's Best Bakery (and Dad has to remind her to order it in the morning).

I said, 'But this means I will not be **SUPREME** and **UNBEATABLE** and Hugo will not be **WILD** with jealousy and Grandma will make the noise!'

Grandma said, 'What noise?'

Mum said, 'Ignore her, Beryl.' Which is when Grandma made the noise.

I said, 'See?'

So Dad said **HE** had an idea and this time it was definitely a **BOBBY DAZZLER** and it was to get Disco Dave to do music and a light show and some Frisbee tricks.

And I could tell Mum was about to do one of her **BIG SIGHS** and say no, but I said, '**PLEASE PLEASE PLEASE!**' really loudly and a lot of times because Madrigal says it is how she got her ears pierced, and **AMAZINGLY** Mum said fine, I can have Disco Dave, but if I want anything else to happen, then I will have to **ORGANISE IT MYSELF**. So now I am **PLEASED AS PUNCH** because I am very **KEEN** on organising. So far me and Nirmal have:

a) written the invitations on three colours of paper and put stamps on the envelopes, only we don't know all the addresses yet so that bit will have to wait.

b) decided that tea will be a barbecue, because there is one in the back of the LAIR and Dad is always saying, 'Looks like nice weather for a barbecue, Jeanie,' but Mum never agrees.

3. asked Dad to check if there is a chocolate fountain in Disco Dave's garage and if not we will invent one.

Plus it is my **ACTUAL** birthday tomorrow and Nirmal says I will probably get a sea monkey, and also Mum says the moustache and beard might have worn off by then, and I can look Grandma in the eye again and Madrigal will stop saying I am **WEIRD**.

Wednesday

10ish

I have not got a sea monkey. I have got:

1. Flip-flops with purple sparkle on them (from Madrigal).

b) A book about Henry VIII (from Lupin).

c) A one-pound coin (from Grandma who

says I must not spend it all at once).

4. Soap that smells of MANDARIN but looks like a CAT (from Hugo and Muriel).

5. A piece of paper saying 'My name is Geoff' with a picture of an axolotl on it (from Mum and Dad). And it is because they have ADOPTED him from Chipping Grimley Zoo.

Hugo Patterson-Dent (who shouldn't even **BE** in my kitchen but was and so was Muriel) said, 'Axolotls are the **CHEAPEST**. I have got a **POLAR BEAR** and Muriel has got a **MARMOSET**.'

So Mum said they had run out of polar bears **AND** marmosets and Geoff was all that was left. And Madrigal said it was also kinder than having an actual pangolin because Geoff is not **ENDANGERED**, although it is **NOT GOOD** that he lives in a **TINY TANK**.

I said, 'When he comes here, he can have the whole **BATH**, now that I am not getting a sea monkey.'

Hugo Patterson-Dent said, 'They don't come to visit you, Daffodil Patterson. They send you letters twice a year and a card at Christmas. Didn't you know that?'

I did **NOT** know that but I did not say so. What I did say was, 'Why are you **EVEN HERE**, Hugo?'

And he said it is because

Olga Romanova (who is their babysitter, and who can do the splits both ways) has got chicken pox and so it is an **EMERGENCY** (because they are only allowed to our house without Aunt Rex in **EMERGENCIES**). And I was about to say this was unfair because it is my birthday when Mum announced it was time to go to Glory Days because it is macaroni cheese day and so Norbert Ogden will **KICK OFF**. And Dad announced he had to go to work and then to Disco Dave's to get my **MYSTERY** present.

Hugo said, 'I hope it is not a Junior Chemistry Set with the labels missing.'

I said, 'I hope it is,' but only to annoy Hugo.

But Dad said it is definitely not, it is better and is a **BOBBY DAZZLER**. And then they were **OFF** to work and Lupin was **OFF** to Beef McKenzie's and Madrigal was **OFF** to Luna Gilhoolie's and so it was just me and Grandma and Muriel and Hugo.

Hugo said, 'Why is there pen on your face, Daffodil Patterson?'

I said, 'It is a **DISGUISE**.'

Only he said, 'It is not, because you do not look like anybody else. You look like Daffodil Patterson with pen on.'

And for once Grandma was **ON MY SIDE** because she said, 'She looks like **GIDEON FITZPATRICK**!' and did a shudder and then went back to the newspaper.

Then Muriel said **SHE** would like to look like Gideon Fitzpatrick.

Hugo said, 'I would not do that if I were you, Muriel Patterson-Dent.'

But Muriel said, 'You are not in charge of me, Hugo Patterson-Dent.'

Which is actually true because Grandma is. So I asked Grandma if we could go to Nirmal's (because that is where the indelible pen is) and she said, 'The sooner the better.' So we are going now.

7ish

Nirmal's house was even **MORE** brilliant than usual because:

1. He and Call-Me-Ariel and Tonks had got me World of Wizard cards for my birthday and we only lost four of them.

b) Call-Me-Ariel let us make pizzas with ANYTHING on them for lunch and so me and Muriel had jam, and Nirmal had peas and mashed potato, and Hugo had cheese and tomato because THAT IS THE RULE.

3. Call-Me-Ariel's friend Bogdan was there who can juggle knives and EAT FIRE while playing the harmonica, and he did ALL THREE and only singed

some curtains and sliced a table a bit.

4. Tonks found some face paint so we did not need to use the INDELIBLE pen and she also found a WIG, so now Muriel looks like Gideon Fitzpatrick with BIG HAIR and we used glue because the wig kept falling off and it is SUPERglue so it will definitely stay on now.

And then we decided to come back to 43 Bean Street to see if we could borrow some fake tattoos from Madrigal because we think Gideon Fitzpatrick definitely has tattoos, and when we got home Dad was already there and so was Disco Dave and so was someone else and it was an **ENORMOUS** dog with long legs and a long face and a red collar.

Hugo said, 'Why is there a dog in the kitchen?'

Dad said, 'It is a **MYSTERY**.'

And Hugo said, 'It is not, it is a greyhound.'

And Dad said, 'Well, yes, but it is a **MYSTERY** present.'

And Muriel went, '**OOH**.'

And Nirmal said, '**OHMYDAYS!**'

And I said, 'My tummy is a **WASHING MACHINE** and I might **EXPLODE!**'

And Dave said, 'Well don't do it all over Colin.'

Because that is the dog's name, and Dad said he used to be the fastest greyhound in Chipping Grimley only now he is retired and needs a good home, and what better home than 43 Bean Street?

Which is when Mum walked in and so did Aunt Rex and neither of them looked pleased.

Mum said, 'Please tell me that dog is not staying, Marv.'

And Dad said, 'I cannot do that. And anyway, it will be a good **EDUCATION**.' Because Mum **DOES NOT MIND** things if they are **EDUCATIONAL**.

And Aunt Rex said, 'Why do you and Muriel look like **HOOLIGANS?**'

JO
COOKIES

D.R.
L.B.
BREAD
GRIM NEWS

I said, 'We do not look like **HOOLIGANS** we look like Gideon Fitzpatrick.'

Aunt Rex's lips went **VERY THIN** and her face went **VERY RED** and she said, 'And **WHO** is Gideon Fitzpatrick?'

And Grandma said, 'A bad, bad man.'

Which is when Aunt Rex said it was time to go home and that this is why it is **EMERGENCIES ONLY** at our house, only not even **EMERGENCIES** are worth it from now on. And Disco Dave said it was probably time he was off as well.

Mum was about to say something about that, only Colin licked her face so she couldn't but when Disco Dave had gone and Colin had finished, she said,

'That is **REVOLTING**, Marv,' and

then she made a lot of rules, which are:

a) Me and Dad have to clean Colin's teeth and give him a bath and when Dad said that might be tricky because of the PLUG SITUATION she said, 'That is a YOU problem, Marv.'

b) Me and Dad have to walk him and pick up his poo because she is NOT doing it UNDER ANY CIRCUMSTANCES.

3. Colin is not allowed on the sofa OR on the beds UNDER ANY CIRCUMSTANCES. Only Dad said what

about EXCEPTIONAL ones like, e.g. if the floor was totally gone. And then they argued for about five million minutes about the meaning of EXCEPTIONAL and in the end Mum said, 'Fine, if the circumstances are that EXCEPTIONAL then he can use the bed or the sofa, but it will NEVER HAPPEN.'

4. If there is any NONSENSE then he will be going back to Disco Dave, MARK HER WORDS.

And me and Dad agreed to all of them and I said this was the

BEST BIRTHDAY EVER and also my party will be **SUPREME** and **UNBEATABLE** because Colin will be there and he is better than a llama.

Thursday

<u>10ish</u>

Colin is definitely **EDUCATIONAL**.

The first thing I have learned is that you can make a plug from a piece of flip-flop with purple sparkle on it. It was my idea because I said the hole would be a **FEATURE** and Nirmal agreed, and so Nirmal cut it out with the **BIG SCISSORS** (because I am not allowed to use them, not after last time) and it fitted exactly into the plughole. Then we ran the taps so the water was right up to the brim to check that the bath wasn't leaky at all and it was **NOT**, which was **EDUCATIONAL**.

Only then it turned out Colin did not fancy getting into the bath. I said I would put on my swimming costume and show him, because when I do not fancy doing things,

Dad does them first to show me it is **FINE** and it usually is. And it worked because as soon as I got in, Colin was **IMMEDIATELY KEEN** and jumped in and a **LOT** of water jumped out. Only Nirmal said it did

not matter because the amount of water was **DOG VOLUME** and if we sucked up the water and measured it we could find out how big Colin is, which is **EDUCATIONAL**.

So we got the hoover and started sucking up the water, only after about ten seconds the hoover made a weird noise and then stopped working. And Nirmal said, 'This proves hoovers do not like sucking water up.' And I agreed and said this was **VERY EDUCATIONAL**.

And then we decided to do another **EDUCATIONAL** thing, which was an **EXPERIMENT** to see what food Colin likes best. The results were that he is **NOT KEEN** on dog food but he **IS** keen on:

1. Cheesy Frizzles.

b) Oxtail soup.

3. Dad's EXTRA HOT SAUCE, which only he can eat because he is BRAVE and also INFLAMMABLE.

4. The custard that Madrigal made two weeks ago and which no one will eat because it has BITS in.

e) His toothbrush.

Which is when Grandma said we should stop feeding him things before he is sick and **DO SOMETHING USEFUL** instead. And we were just about to see if Colin could wash the kitchen floor with his tongue, which would be **SUPER**

useful because of the bit where we spilt all the **EXTRA HOT SAUCE**, when Aunt Rex rang and did some shouting because Muriel's wig is still stuck on, and Hugo's waterproof watch that is accurate to a **NANOSECOND** has gone missing and so it is **INEVITABLY** somewhere at our

house in among **ALL THE MAYHEM**.

So I said, 'Do not worry, I will find it for you.'

She said, 'I am worried,' and, 'This time please **USE YOUR EYES**,' and then hung up.

But me and Nirmal and Colin are going to **PROVE HER WRONG** because we will **USE OUR EYES** and also Colin will **USE HIS NOSE** because dogs are good at sniffing for things like bombs and waterproof watches that are accurate to a **NANOSECOND**.

6ish

Colin has not sniffed out Hugo's waterproof watch that is accurate to a **NANOSECOND** but on the **BRIGHT SIDE** he has sniffed out:

1. A very dead beetle with only four legs left.

b) A sausage from the time Dad tried to prove he could catch a sausage in his mouth and he could not.

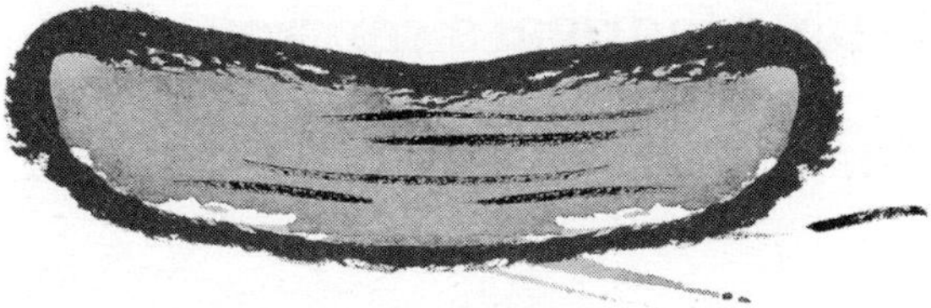

3. The RED WIZARD from the World of Wizard board game, which Madrigal said I had STOLEN because it is her favourite, but I had not, I had just hidden it under something, only I forgot what.

On the **GLOOMY** side, he has eaten the very dead beetle and the sausage, plus possibly Madrigal's second-best socks, which have **BEES** on them, and Lupin's lucky plectrum, because they are all missing, and so now they are both in **MOODS**.

I said it might not have been Colin, it could have been, e.g. Luna Gilhoolie or Beef McKenzie or Grandma. Only Lupin said Beef McKenzie hasn't even been to 43 Bean Street today because he is cross about Meat Parlour. And Madrigal said Luna Gilhoolie hasn't even been to 43 Bean Street today because she is cross about something to do with Paris 2, i.e. Paris Mears (Paris Grout is Paris 1 because she is taller and louder and her birthday is first). And Mum said Grandma won't even eat pizza because of it being **SUSPICIOUS** so she is hardly likely to eat **SOCKS**. And then Colin was sick on the kitchen floor and there was a sock in it and a plectrum and also a plastic frog that I once lost under the sofa, so Lupin said **ALL EVIDENCE** points to the dog. Which is when Mum said Dad has to wash the socks and the plectrum and the frog and also if his behaviour doesn't improve by this time tomorrow then he will be going back to Disco Dave.

Dad said, 'Me or the dog?'

Mum said, 'Do not tempt me, Marv,' and also, '**HOW MANY TIMES**, Daffodil? The dog is **NOT** allowed on the sofa. Especially not when he smells of **CHEESY SICK**.'

So I got Colin off the sofa and **DEFINITELY NOT** on to my bed. And I am not worried because me and Nirmal will do **TRAINING** and so by this time tomorrow Colin's behaviour will probably be **AMAZING**.

Friday

4ish

Things Colin cannot do:

1. Sit.

b) Lie down.

c) Roll over.

4. Shake a paw.

5. Catch a ball in his mouth.

Things Colin can do:

a) Catch a sausage in his mouth.

b) Catch a cheese sandwich in his mouth.

3. Catch some EXTRA HOT SAUCE in his mouth and only get some on the floor.

Also he has broken the door of the washing machine, and unravelled all Grandma's wool from her knitting, and chewed the remote control for the television.

I said at least he didn't actually **EAT** the remote control, but Grandma says the television is stuck on **CHURCH** channel so she cannot watch the horse racing any more and has to watch Reverend Beddoes, and Reverend Beddoes is worse than Gideon Fitzpatrick and even Mum agreed and she does not even know who Gideon Fitzpatrick is. She says **THE MINUTE** Dad gets home Colin is going **STRAIGHT**

BACK to Disco Dave's, and no I **CANNOT** have another pet, because I have Geoff the axolotl, or had I forgotten?

I said I had not forgotten, and actually I am going to write him a letter **THIS MINUTE** in my bedroom and so is Nirmal.

Only now we cannot do it because we are too **FULL OF GLOOM** and so is Colin and so we are all lying on my bed but it is all right because these are definitely **EXCEPTIONAL CIRCUMSTANCES**.

6ish

Dad is home and it turns out Colin **CANNOT** go **STRAIGHT BACK** to Disco Dave's because Disco Dave has gone to somewhere called West Bootley to play Frisbee all weekend. Mum said this sounded very **CONVENIENT** and Dad said actually it is not convenient because West Bootley is **MILES** away.

Mum said, 'Fine, but that dog is in **LAST CHANCE SALOON**, Marv. **MARK MY WORDS**.' And Dad said they were marked.

But I said, 'Disco Dave **WILL** be back in time to do music and a light show and Frisbee tricks for my party, won't he?'

And Dad said, 'Probably.' Which

usually means **NO**, and Mum said so.

But Dad said, '**DO NOT WORRY** I have the perfect replacement.' And it is Vigorous Pigeon/Meat Parlour/Hairy Wasp and he will ask Lupin when he gets back from Oscar Boggins's house.

Madrigal said but they haven't even played **ONE** concert yet, and Dad said then it will be even better, because that means my party will **GO DOWN IN HISTORY**.

Mum said, 'Let's hope not.'

But she said it quietly and anyway me and Nirmal decided we would quite like to **GO DOWN IN HISTORY** and so would Colin, because we will definitely be **SUPREME** and **UNBEATABLE** then.

Saturday

10ish

Now we are less **FULL OF GLOOM**, me and Colin have written a letter to Geoff the axolotl and it goes like this:

43 Bean Street

Chipping Grimley

Essex

Dear Geoff

My name is Daffodil Patterson and I live at 43 Bean Street (the rest of the address that I can remember is at the top of the letter so you can use that to write back but you'll have to look up the postcode. I think it has a G in it). I just got a dog called Colin for my birthday as well as you but he is in LAST CHANCE SALOON even though these are EXCEPTIONAL CIRCUMSTANCES. Also I have a lot of questions, i.e.

1. What is the best thing about being an axolotl?

b) What do worms taste like to you? Because me and Nirmal tried some of Dad's when he went fishing with Uncle Malcolm once and they did not taste of NICE.

c) Do you have a last name and if not do you want to be Patterson?

Love

Daffodil and Colin Patterson

And then
Colin licked
the envelope and I
stuck it down and
we went to post it in
the letter box outside
Norman Fazackerley's
house at number 37.
On the way Colin got
VERY INTERESTED
in Measles, who is
Norman's cat (and
who once bit me)
and tried to

climb in the window to meet her. But I said, '**DO NOT** do that, Colin! You are in **LAST CHANCE SALOON**! And also Measles will **EAT YOU**.'

And he actually did **NOT** do it and so I was going to tell Mum that he is almost out of the saloon now, only when we got back Mum and Dad had had another **TO-DO** and it was because of the birthday cake, i.e. she said Dad did not remind her to order a cake from Barry's Best Bakery only Dad said he **DID** remind her but she was busy with Lupin's shoes (but not because he is vegetarian. It is because he has one foot a size bigger than the other so he has **DIFFICULT** feet).

She said, 'So I reminded you to remind me again and you did not remind me that time.'

And Dad said that is because by then **HE** was busy with Lupin's shoes so if you think about it, it's Lupin's fault for having **DIFFICULT** feet. And Mum did think about it and decided it is **NOT** Lupin's fault it is Dad's, because Lupin inherited the **DIFFICULT** feet from Dad and also because of the not-reminding.

Which is when I said, 'So **IS** there cake?'

Mum said, 'Ask your dad.'

So I did and he said, 'Yes there is definitely cake and it is going to be the **BEST CAKE EVER** because we will make it and it will be **FIVE LAYERS** and have **SPARKLY ICING**, just you wait and see!'

Mum said she would rather not wait and see and please could he just get a cake from Barry even if it is fruit cake.

But Dad said, 'No one likes fruit cake because of the **BITS** and anyway, **WHO IS TO SAY** I am not the next **CELEBRITY BAKER**?'

Mum was definitely about to say that he was **NOT** the next **CELEBRITY BAKER** but that is when Grandma fell off the chair because the leg was wobbly.

Mum gave me a hard stare, but I said, 'The leg was wobbly even **BEFORE** Colin chewed it.'

And Dad said, 'Perhaps we should make ourselves **SCARCE**, Daff.' Which means go somewhere else.

And so we are and it is next door to Nirmal's, and we are going to make a cake and also invent a chocolate fountain because I remembered I never asked Disco Dave if there was one in the garage and now he is in West Bootley.

4ish

We have not invented a chocolate

fountain because Call-Me-Ariel says we need a special pump to do that and no we cannot have the one from the tropical fish tank on the landing, because it will have **POO** in it, and also the fish need it and they are as important as candles for all the **THERAPY**. On the **BRIGHT** side, Tonks says she will melt a bowl of chocolate in the microwave and we can roast marshmallows on the barbecue and then dip them in it and it will be **JUST AS GOOD** and I agreed.

Also we have made a cake and it **IS** the **BEST CAKE EVER**

and Dad says it is thanks to his **INVENTING** skills and Tonks's **ART** skills and also the **CUPBOARDS OF PLENTY** (because the ones in Nirmal's house have actual cake ingredients in them and ours mainly have tins of beans and crisps).

It has five layers and they go like this:

1. Vanilla.

2. Rhubarb.

c) Clementine.

4. Cream cheese and chive (because Tonks says it is important to be EXPERIMENTAL with art and cooking is actually a kind of art).

5. Blackcurrant.

And on top is green and pink icing with magic space powder sprinkles that fizz in your mouth when you eat it, and also the plastic frog that Colin found, and a ballerina with only one leg missing and the Wizard Wangle card, which is the best World of Wizard card, and it represents **WHATEVER YOU WANT** because Tonks says that is the best thing about art.

Madrigal says it looks like a unicorn has exploded and Mum says she is not sure the cream cheese and chive layer will go down well with Aunt Rex, and

Grandma says it had better not have **BITS** in **ANY** layer. But I say it is the **BEST CAKE EVER** and will make my party **SUPREME** and **UNBEATABLE**.

Sunday

8ish

Something **TERRIBLE** has happened, i.e. the cake is **GONE**, even the plastic frog and the ballerina with only one leg missing and the Wizard Wangle card! Dad said perhaps **CAKE THIEVES** smelt how amazing it was and broke into our kitchen and stole it last night while we were all sleeping. But Mum said:

1. Colin is looking GREEN ABOUT THE GILLS, i.e. sick, so all fingers point to him.
b) If it WAS cake thieves then Colin should have barked but he did not so it is still all the fault of Colin.

Grandma said it was **NOT FAIR** to blame Colin, because he is only a dog and therefore does not know any better and actually it was probably **SOMEONE ELSE'S** fault because it **ALWAYS IS** at 43 Bean Street, e.g. perhaps it is Madrigal's fault for leaving the kitchen door open **AGAIN**.

But Madrigal said perhaps it is Lupin's fault for not putting the cake in the **FRIDGE** like Mum told him to.

Lupin said perhaps it is Mum's fault for having **VEGETABLES** in the fridge for once taking up **VITAL CAKE ROOM** so that he was forced to leave it on the table.

Mum said it is actually Dad's fault for getting Colin in the first place.

Dad said it is actually Mum's fault for not making Colin feel welcome and that he probably ate the cake because of the **HOLE OF SADNESS** inside him, because Call-Me-Ariel once said that is why Dad eats so many crisps.

And then he and Mum had another **TO-DO** until they agreed it was definitely Colin's fault after all and Mum has shut him in the **LAIR** for the moment so he cannot do any more damage and he is definitely going back to Disco Dave's in the morning. I said they have **RUINED** my birthday and now I am **FULL OF GLOOM**. But Dad said on the plus side the day **CANNOT GET ANY WORSE** and he will bet me a pound that it does not.

11ish

The day **HAS** got worse, i.e. Lupin's band Vigorous Pigeon has totally broken up.

Mum said this was the **LIMIT** and couldn't they wait until tomorrow to make that decision and just play, e.g. three songs this afternoon at the party? But Lupin says the **ARTISTIC DIFFERENCES** are too **ENORMOUS** and it is a solo career for him from now on. Nirmal (who had come round to share the **GLOOM**) said he could join in on recorder and he wouldn't mind being called Meat Parlour but Lupin says he is just going to lie in the dark in his room for a bit and sigh.

Dad said on the **BRIGHT** side he now owes me a pound, and he will bet me another that the Lupin **HOO-HA** is the **END** of the **GETTING WORSE**.

3ish

Dad owes me another pound. It is because when I asked Mum what time my three friends, i.e. Beavis Meek (even though we are not speaking to him until he admits that green is the best Tooty Chew flavour) and Fenton Eggs (who is second toughest in Year 4) and Elsie Brain (who once licked a worm for a dare) were arriving, she said, 'I don't know, Daff. What time did you **TELL** them to arrive when you telephoned them?'

And I said, 'I did not **TELEPHONE** them, I wrote it on special invitations!'

Mum said, 'But not in invisible ink this time?' Because last time I did do this and no one understood anything because they are not **SUPER SPIES** like me and Nirmal.

And I said, 'No, in extra special **VISIBLE** ink.' Because it was Madrigal's best gel pen.

And Mum said, 'And did anyone **ACCEPT** the invitations?'

And I thought for a **NANOSECOND** and said, 'Not actually **OUT LOUD**.'

And Mum said, 'And you did

remember to **SEND** the invitations,

didn't you?'

And that was when

my tummy

did a

swoop like

when Dad drives

over a humpback bridge too fast, because I realised that I hadn't remembered to send them because I hadn't remembered to get the addresses, because I was too excited about Colin. And so then I was **DOUBLY GLOOMY** because of

Colin leaving and no friends coming and I said so.

And Mum did a sigh and said, 'Don't worry. It's a Sunday and **NOTHING** happens on a Sunday especially not in the summer holidays and I will telephone them **RIGHT NOW** and it will be **FINE**.'

Only it was not **FINE** because it turns out **LOTS** of things are happening on a Sunday, i.e.

1. Beavis Meek is at his gran's house in Benidorm.

b) Fenton Eggs is at his uncle's house in Bury St Edmunds (which is a real place, me and Nirmal checked).

c) Elsie Brain is in somewhere called Woking (only not at anyone's house, she is just there and no one knows why, not even her).

So then it was just me and Nirmal and Madrigal. Only Madrigal said actually she was going to Luna Gilhoolie's because they have made up about Paris 2, i.e. Paris Mears, and are going to make friendship bracelets to **PROVE** it. Which is when Aunt Rex arrived with Hugo and Muriel and a cardboard box with a **CAKE** in it.

Dad said, 'Why the cardboard box with a **CAKE** in it, Rex, don't you trust me?'

And she said, 'Not particularly, Marvin. Plus this house is like a **BLACK HOLE** because of **ALL THE MAYHEM** so heaven knows what might have happened to it.'

And Hugo said, 'Black holes mean everything disappears,

Daffodil Patterson, e.g. my waterproof watch that is accurate to a nanosecond.'

And I said I **KNEW** that (because of the time me and Nirmal were practising to be astronauts getting sucked into a black hole, i.e. the cupboard under the stairs, and I got a ventilated hamster ball stuck on my head).

Hugo said, 'Our cake is six layers and is made with seventeen actual lemons and it has swirls on top that are real gold. And where even is your cake, Daffodil Patterson?'

And I was about to say 'inside the shed', which wasn't even a lie because it was inside Colin who was inside the shed, when there was a massive **CRASH** and when we looked out of the window the shed had **COLLAPSED** and Colin was **GONE**!

And he is still gone now and **NO ONE** can find him. Which is why me and Nirmal are in my bedroom writing this and doing sighing, instead of in the kitchen listening to Mum and Dad having another **TO-DO** because she has been telling him about the shed for MONTHS and he **DID NOT LISTEN**, and Hugo saying, 'I told you so, Daffodil Patterson,' and Grandma doing the noise like a broken vacuum cleaner and calling us **CATASTROPHE PATTERSONS**.

Aunt Rex is right, i.e. this house **IS** a **BLACK HOLE** because of **ALL THE MAYHEM**, and I do not blame Colin for running away and in fact I am going to pack my purple rucksack with the clippy thing and the water-bottle holder and run away too because it **CANNOT BE WORSE** than 43 Bean Street.

4ish

We cannot find my purple rucksack with the clippy thing and the water-bottle holder (because we think it might be at Nirmal's house from when we were training to be **POLAR EXPLORERS** by seeing how long we could stand in a cold bath with rucksacks on and it was about an hour) so we have packed Dad's wheelie suitcase with only one wheel broken that he got from Disco Dave with:

1. The flip-flops with purple sparkle on them and the hole from where we made the plug.

b) The book about Henry VIII.

c) The one-pound coin from Grandma (because Dad still owes me the others).

d) The soap that smells of MANDARIN but looks like a CAT.

5. The piece of paper with the picture of the axolotl on it saying 'My name is Geoff'.

6. The World of Wizard cards (even though there are five missing now including the Wizard Wangle card, which is the best one).

g) A photograph of Colin looking surprised, which Dad took with his instant camera that he got off Disco Dave before it broke (which Mum said was only a matter of time until it happened and it was).

The zip of the suitcase doesn't quite shut (from when me and Nirmal tested it to see if I could fit inside and be wheeled up and down the garden without falling out, and I can't) but I have tied a pair of Madrigal's tights around it, which is very **RESOURCEFUL** and so I would be a good **POLAR EXPLORER** after all. Only now Mum is knocking on the door, so I will find out what she wants first and it is probably to **HAVE WORDS**, and then I will definitely be running away.

8ish

Mum did not want to **HAVE WORDS**. She said she had an idea, which was that she and me and Nirmal and Hugo and Muriel were going to **HUNT HIGH AND LOW** around Chipping Grimley until we found Colin.

I asked what Dad and Aunt Rex were going to do.

She said, 'They're going to hold the fort here with Grandma, in case Colin comes back by himself.'

And I said this was actually a **BOBBY DAZZLER** of an idea and I got my flip-flops with purple sparkle on them out of the suitcase.

Mum said, 'You do know those have got a massive hole in them?'

I said, 'I do. It is a feature.'

And Mum agreed. And then we were off with me in front, and then Nirmal and Mum, and then Hugo and Muriel.

Hugo said, 'I do not see why **YOU** are in front, Daffodil Patterson. You are not the **GROWN-UP**.'

I said, 'But I know Colin **BEST** so I will know where he will have gone.'

Mum said, 'Where **HAS** he gone, Daff?'

I thought very hard about what Colin likes to do and number one was **EAT THINGS**, so I said we should go to Paradise City, because they sell Cheesy Frizzles and Oxtail Soup, and in the **EXPERIMENT** they were Colin's favourite.

Hugo said, 'He will not be there, Daffodil Patterson. You will see.'

But Mum said he **MIGHT BE** so off we trooped.

Only when we got to Paradise City there was **NO SIGN** of Colin, and Beef McKenzie, who was behind the counter, said no dogs had been in all afternoon except Bits Pringle's labradoodle, Mince.

Hugo said, 'I told you so, Daffodil Patterson.'

And I was about to say something when Beef said actually his shift had just finished, and he would come and help us look.

'Where next?' said Mum.

And this time me **AND** Nirmal thought very hard about what Colin likes to do and we remembered it is to **UNRAVEL WOOL**, only Madrigal

Paradise City
Paradise City
Chipping Grimley
43
Bean Street
ER

37

had taken it to Luna Gilhoolie's house to make friendship bracelets and so I said we should go there.

Hugo said, 'He will not be there, Daffodil Patterson. You will see.'

But Mum said he **MIGHT BE** so off we trooped again.

Only when we got to Luna Gilhoolie's there was **NO SIGN** of Colin, and Luna said the only animals in her house were **WOODLICE** because she does not believe in keeping pets not even ones that are **FREE TO ROAM**.

Hugo said, 'I told you so, Daffodil Patterson.'

And I was about to say something when Madrigal said they had finished making friendship bracelets and would come and help us look.

'Where next?' said Mum.

And this time **EVERYONE** thought very hard about what Colin likes to do but we couldn't come up with **ANYTHING** else.

I said, 'This is the **WORST BIRTHDAY PARTY EVER**! Colin is probably a **MILLION** miles away by now and he will have nothing to eat but **GRASS** and **CRISP PACKETS**.' Because he likes to lick the insides.

Muriel said, 'Or he could catch a cat.'

And that is when I had my next **BOBBY DAZZLER** and shouted, 'Measles!'

Hugo said, 'Dogs can't get measles. Did you not know that, Daffodil Patterson?'

I said, 'Not **MEASLES** measles. **MEASLES THE CAT**!' Because

Colin was very **KEEN** on Measles when we walked past number 37, i.e. Norman Fazackerley's house.

Hugo said, 'He will not be there, Daffodil Patterson. You will see.'

But Mum said he **MIGHT BE** and so off we trooped yet again. And all the time my insides were jiggling and my head was **FULL OF FEAR** and **EXCITEMENT**, which Call-Me-Ariel says are almost the same thing. And it turns out I was RIGHT to be so full because when we got to Norman Fazackerley's house, **THERE** was Measles staring out of the window, and **THERE** was **COLIN**, staring back!

'Colin!' I shouted, and he turned around and even though he was still looking **GREEN ABOUT THE GILLS**, he was so pleased to see me he licked my face and was not even a bit sick!

'Well done, Daff,' said Mum.

And I said, 'Thank you, and also thank you for helping me look even though you do not like Colin, not even **ONE BIT**.'

She said, 'But I do love you, Daff.'

And my insides felt jiggly again but I did not say so because I was too busy being licked by Colin.

But that's not even the best bit. Because when we got back to 43 Bean Street the garden was already **JAM-PACKED** with people, i.e. Aunt Rex and Uncle Malcolm, and Call-Me-Ariel and Tonks, and Dad and Grandma, and Lupin and Oscar Boggins (who had come round to try to get the band back together), and Disco Dave (who had been disqualified from the Frisbee competition for an illegal combination). And in the middle of them was a big pyramid of wood.

Mum said, 'What is that, Marv? Please don't tell me it's the lair.'

Dad said he could not do that, but he could tell her it was **DAFFODIL'S BIRTHDAY BONFIRE** because he knew that I wanted a party that was **SUPREME** and **UNBEATABLE** and this way it might be.

And it was, because we had:

1. The biggest bonfire that Bean Street has EVER SEEN and we roasted marshmallows on it (because the barbecue had got squished) and had a contest to see who could fit the most in their mouth at once and it was Dad who managed twenty-two. And Mum said, 'At least that will keep him quiet for a bit.' Only it did not because then he swallowed them and said WHO IS TO SAY he will not become a marshmallow-eating PHENOMENOM and make his fortune?

b) A cake with SIX layers made

with SEVENTEEN ACTUAL LEMONS and the SWIRLS on top were REAL GOLD. And everyone except Hugo agreed it probably wasn't as good as one with five layers and green and pink icing with magic space powder sprinkles that fizz in your mouth when you eat them, and a plastic frog and a ballerina with only one leg missing and a Wizard Wangle card, but it was JOLLY GOOD ANYWAY.

c) Vigorous Pigeon's FIRST EVER concert, i.e. Lupin and Oscar Boggins and Beef McKenzie playing a song called 'The Shed is Dead', and Call-Me-Ariel and Nirmal doing interpretive dance to it. Dad says it will GO DOWN IN HISTORY and Hugo says it will NOT but Dad says Hugo does not understand MODERN MUSIC like he does, and WHO IS TO SAY he will not become a FAMOUS BAND MANAGER now and make his fortune?

4. Colin, who is definitely staying, because Disco Dave says he is thinking of investing in GEESE and becoming a GOOSE MAGNATE, and so he cannot have him back because geese and dogs DO NOT MIX.

Colin

VIGOROUS Pigeon

Monday

11ish

It is back to **NORMAL SERVICE** at 43 Bean Street, i.e. Dad is busy being a postman, Mum is busy at Glory Days Care Home with all the old people, Lupin is busy in his bedroom with Beef McKenzie and Oscar Boggins, Madrigal is busy being **ANNOYING**, and Grandma is busy **MINDING HER OWN BUSINESS** and so no one is noticing me and I am **UTTERLY FORGOTTEN**.

But I do not care because:

1. My party was SUPREME and UNBEATABLE after all.

b) Colin has just been sick and in it were the plastic frog, AND the ballerina with only one leg missing, AND the Wizard Wangle card, AND the waterproof watch that is accurate to a NANOSECOND, only it is not accurate at all any more to even a MINUTE so Aunt Rex says I can keep it.

c) I have just had a BOBBY DAZZLER of an idea, and it is to become a DOG DETECTIVE and USE MY EYES to find missing pets, and this one cannot POSSIBLY go wrong.

THE WORST CLASS IN THE WORLD

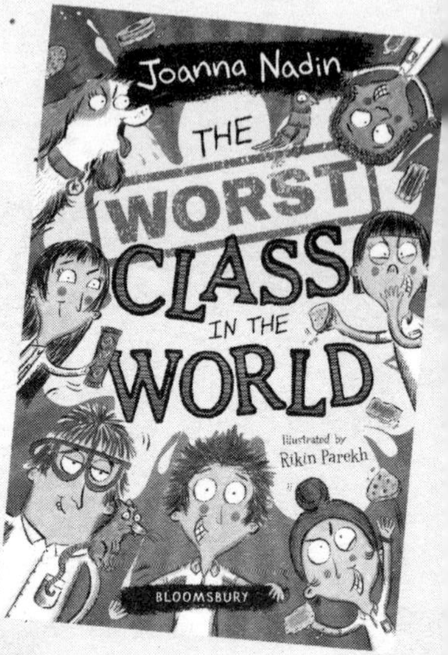

READ THE WHOLE DIABOLICALLY DISASTROUS SERIES!

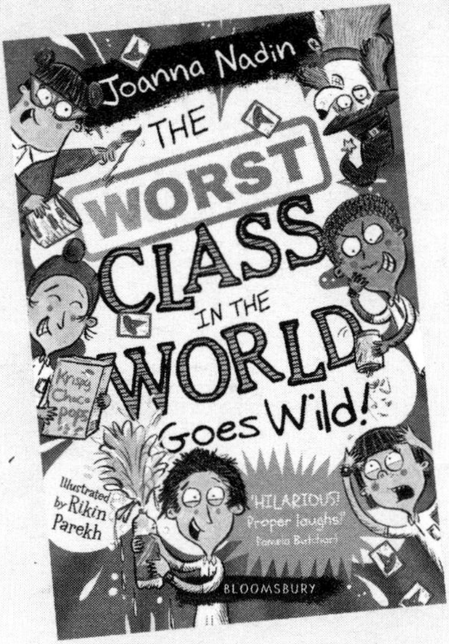

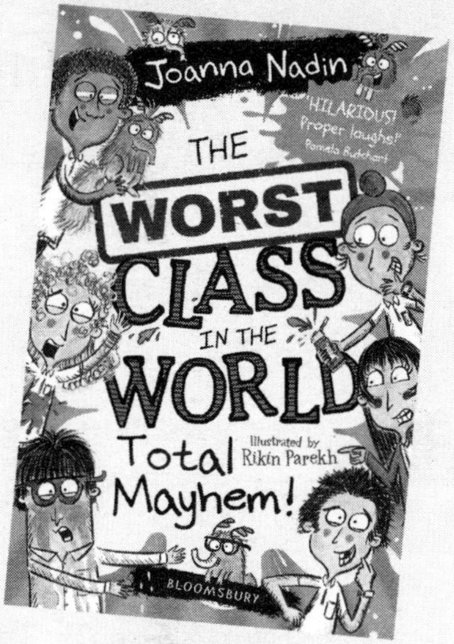

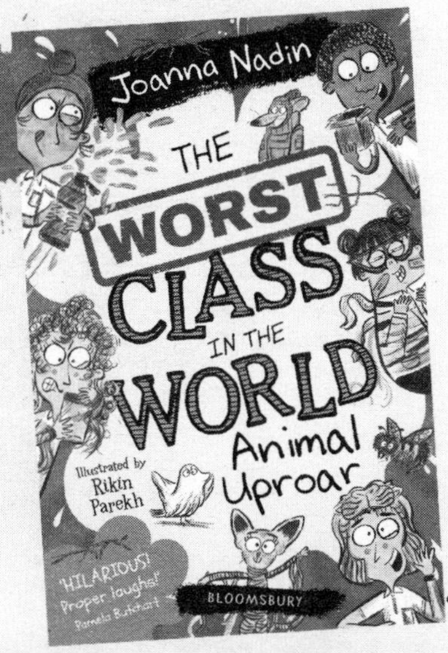

AVAILABLE NOW!

Joanna Nadin is an award-winning author who has written more than ninety books for children. She has also been a juggler, a lifeguard and an adviser to the Prime Minister. Her worst birthday ever was the one when bigger boys and girls INVADED her party and spilt olive oil on the curtains and someone did sick on a wall. She lives in Bath and her favourite things are goats, monkeys and crisps.

Rikin Parekh (aka Mr Rik) is an author/illustrator and ninja. He also works in primary schools as an LSA and worked as a bookseller (which was REALLY, REALLY fun!). His worst birthday ever was when he suffered a seriously bad headache and had to spend all day in bed and miss all the pizza! He lives in Wembley and his favourite things are pizza, dogs, and picking his nose and collecting the bogeys.

Look out for the next **MADCAP** adventure in this brilliantly funny series about Daffodil Patterson

COMING SOON!